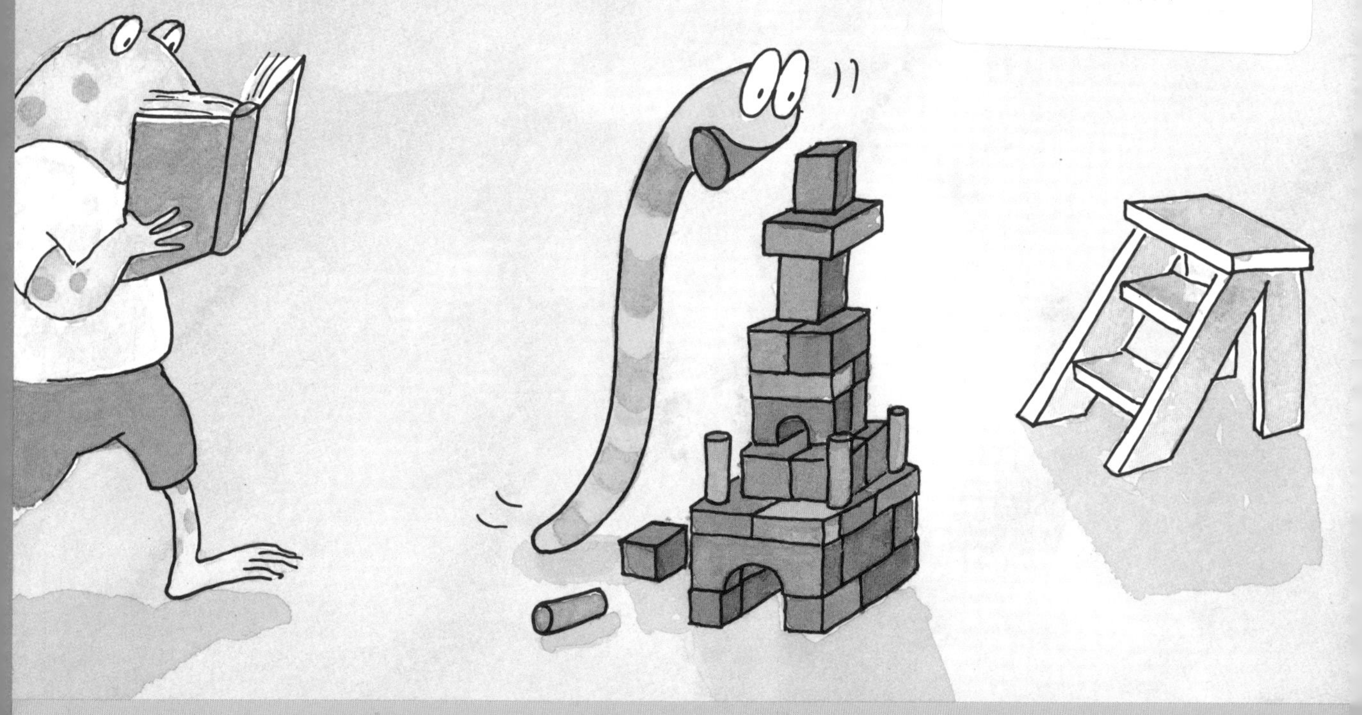

Worm builds a tower.

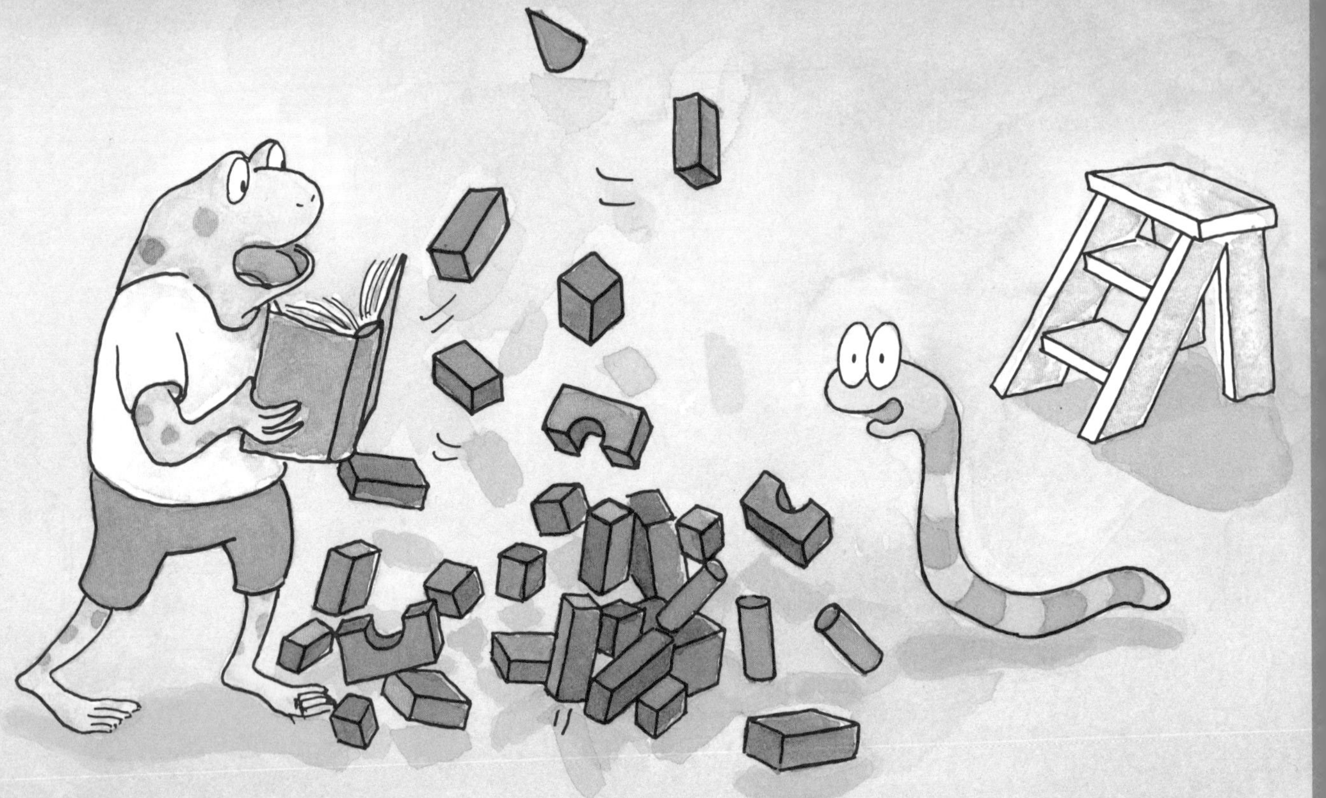

Frog knocks it down.

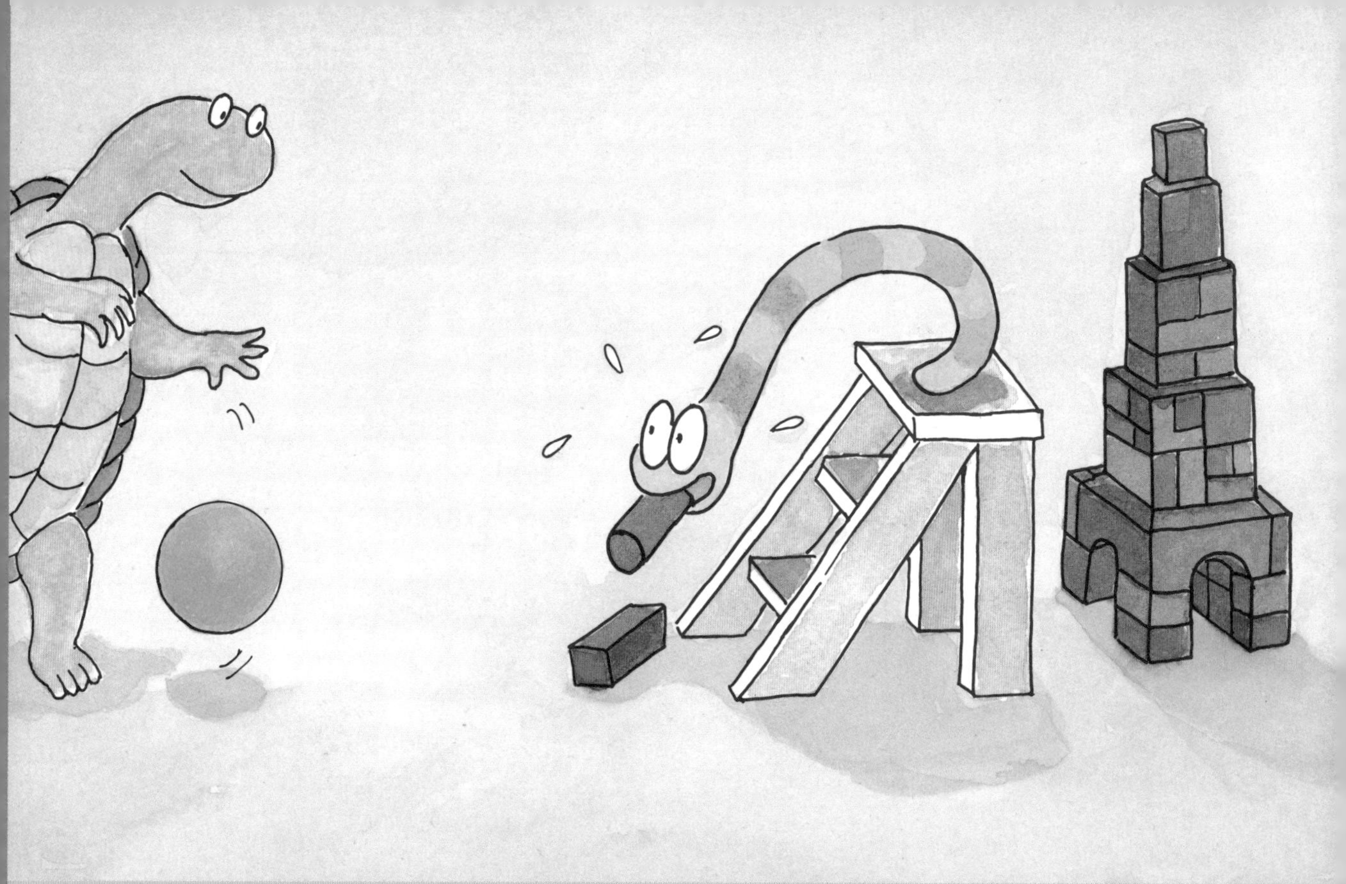

Worm builds a tower.

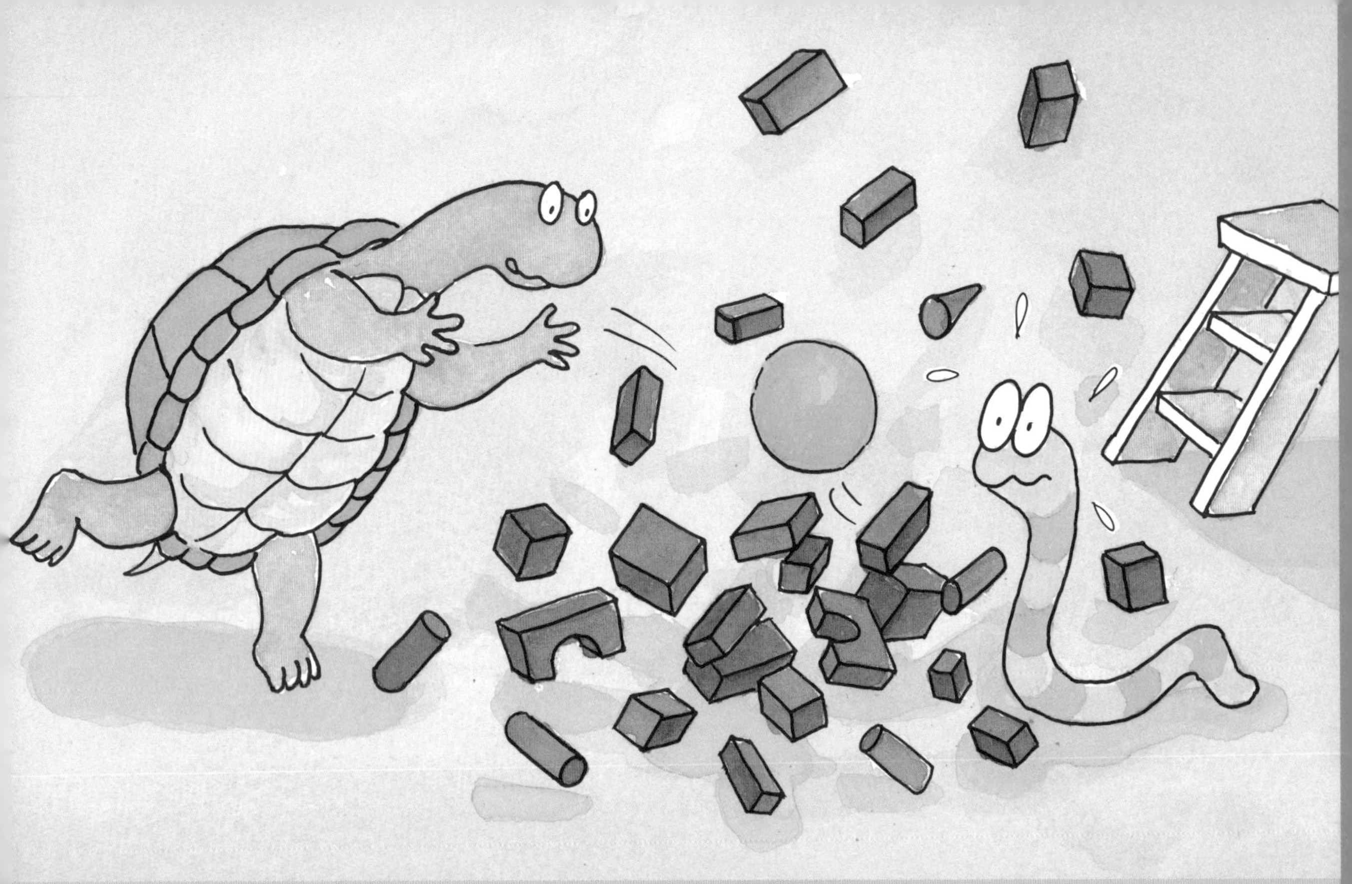

Turtle knocks it down.

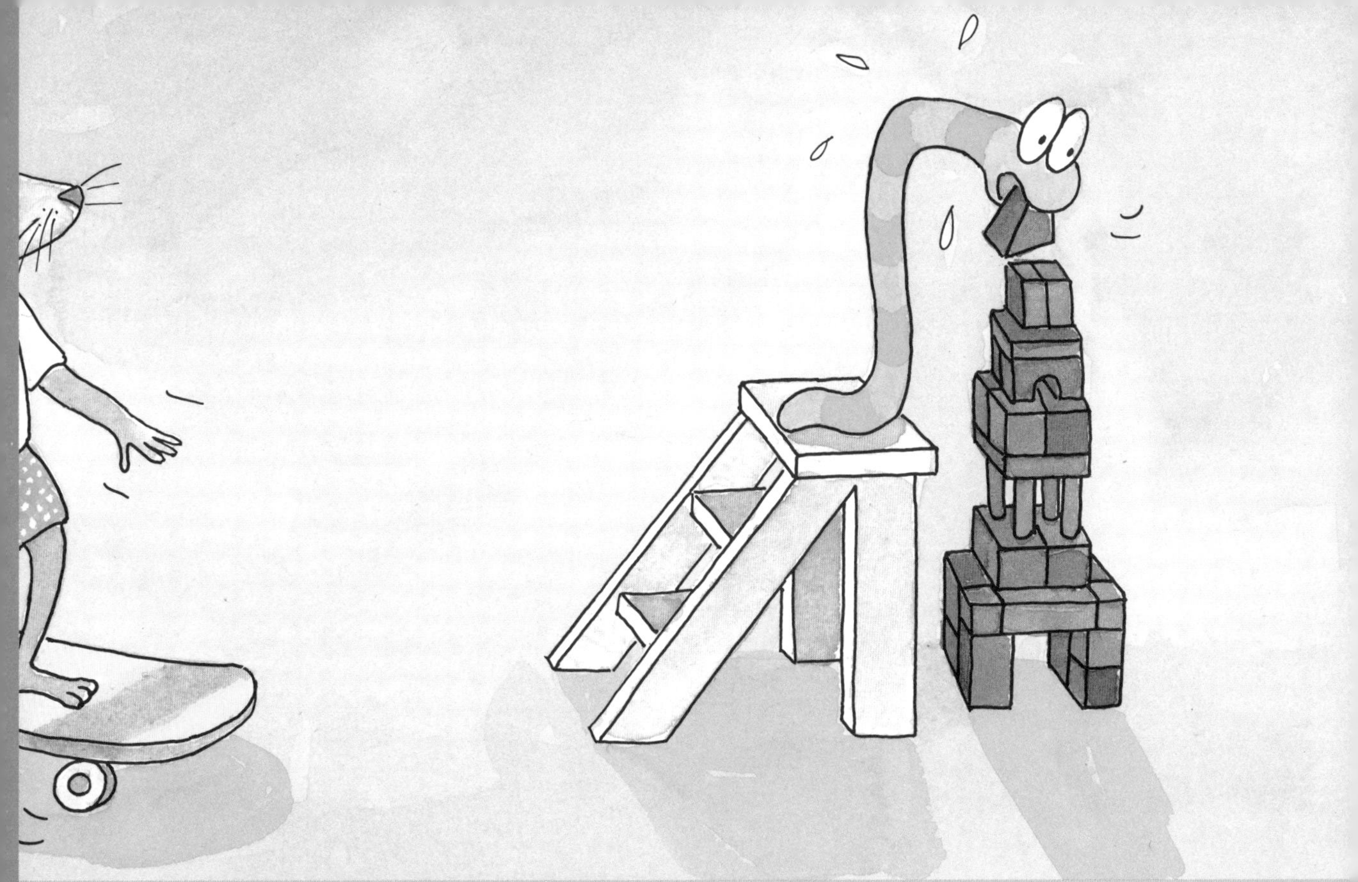

Worm builds a tower.

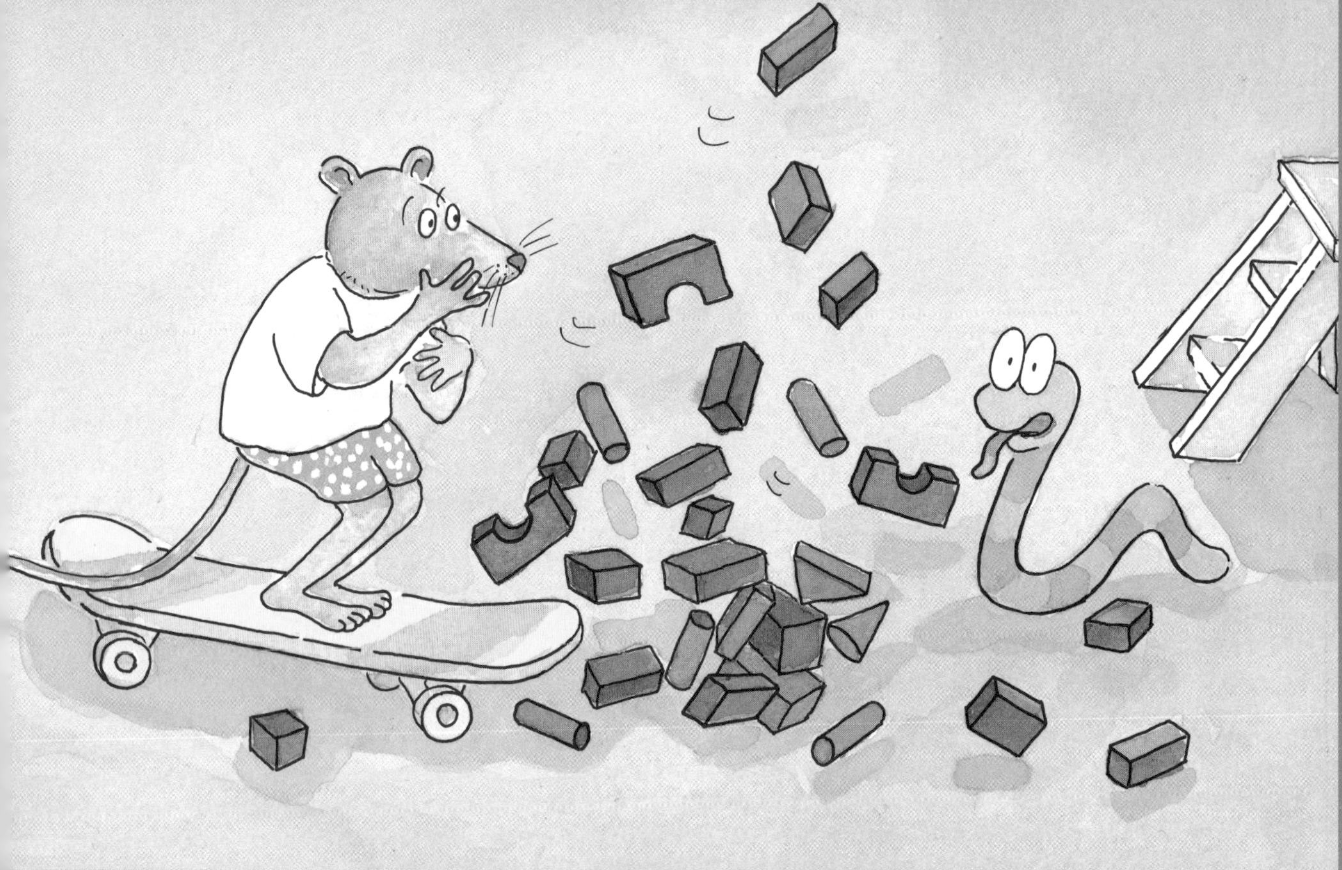

Rat knocks it down.

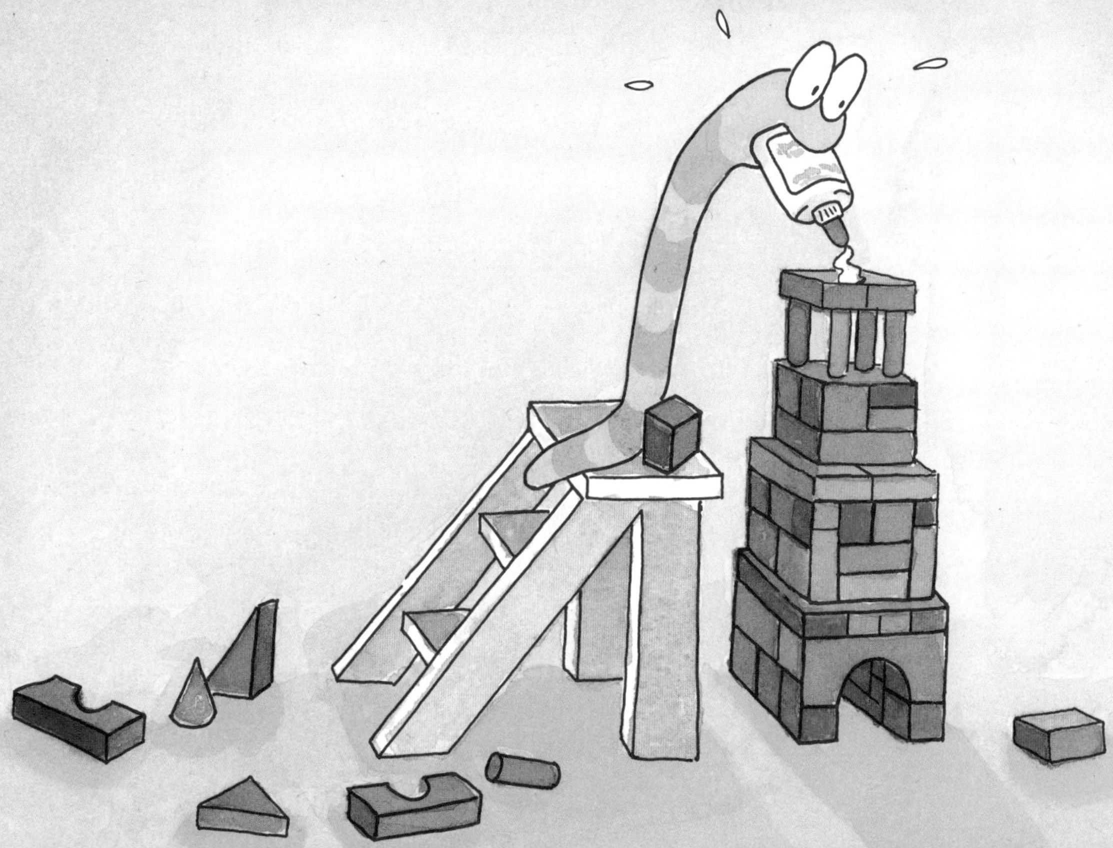

Worm uses glue.

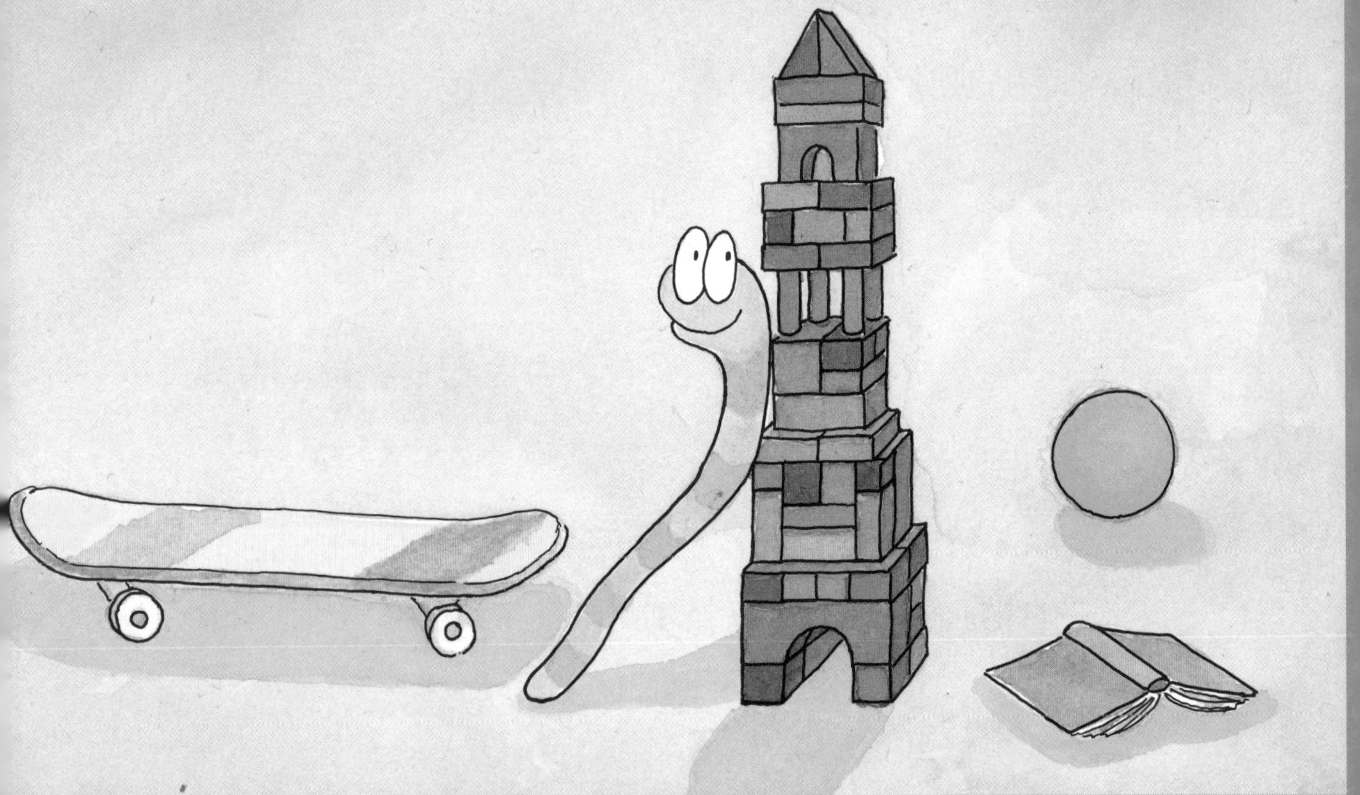

Worm's tower stays up.